Mall Flower

Poems and Short Fiction

Tina Barry

ISBN: 978-0-9965405-1-3

Printed in the United States of America

Cover Design: Kyle Schruder
Front Cover Photo: Bob Barry
Back Cover Photo: Bob Barry

Big Table Publishing Company
Boston, MA
www.bigtablepublishing.com

Thanks to the publications in which some of these poems first appeared, sometimes in slightly different forms:

5 X 5 Literary Magazine: "Bird-watching"
52/250: "To Wed"
Boston Literary Magazine: "A New Tattoo"
Blue Fifth Notebook: "Find Me"
Camroc Press Review: "Swing", "Mall Flower", "Continuing Ed.",
    "Peonies", "Chanukah" and "Table Talk"
Drunken Boat: "Party at My Place"
Flash Frontier: "What's All This?"
Inch Magazine: "Bon Voyage"
The Lascaux Review: "Three Bedrooms in New Jersey"
The Light Ekphrastic: "Honeycomb" and "Her Hair, a Braid"
The Linnets Wings: "It's fine, Mother"
TheNewer York: "The Shopkeeper"
Lost in Thought Magazine: "Float to Water"
MadHat Lit: "Wool and Spool"
Naugatuck River Review: "White Legs"
The Orange Room Review: "Her Hair, a Braid"
Ramshackle Review: "Tuscaloosa"
Short, Fast & Deadly: "One Bag of Popcorn"
THIS Magazine: "No Word for Enchantment"
Yes, Poetry: "Your Last Rooster"

Contents

With love and gratitude to my mother Rosalind Ehlin,
who is nothing like the mothers in *Mall Flower*.

Three Bedrooms

Going South

We left suburban New Jersey

Our last trip to Miami before Dad switched families. My younger sister and I filled in every Mad Libs blank with "tits" and "ass" so Mom would yell and make noise in the car.

At a lunch counter in Pennsylvania, the waitress asked a man with a Popeye tattoo if he wanted a plate of spinach. It was the only time Dad laughed.

At a motel in Delaware

My sister held my head underwater in the swimming pool. I heard shadowy sounds, then the glug of a motor working unnoticed.

At night we peeled back the synthetic quilts on our beds. From my parents' bed: Mom's restless feet. I watched my sister not sleep.

The woman in the motel's office read palms. Mom had a short love line.

In Georgia

A giant peach teetered like a swooning moon atop a water tower. We bought gifts in a roadside shop: A bikini patterned with peaches. Straws filled with peach-flavored sugar. We sprinkled the coral grains over our stuffed animals' fur. They looked glamorous twinkling in the moonlight.

Dad slowed down to watch cotton pickers bowed in the heat. They stared back.

Beside the pool

At the pool in the hotel in Miami, we sipped Shirley Temples, took turns curled beside Dad on a blue-striped chaise lounge. I smacked my sister's face. She had taken too long raking the hair on Dad's legs with a doll's comb.

Dad wouldn't take us to Sea World, so Mom bought dolphin-shaped pool floats and took pictures.

Returning to Jersey

My sister threw a deck of cards out the car window. We watched them spiral tightly together down the highway, then blink out like dead stars as the wind drew them apart.

Bon Voyage

We've gathered on the dock. Mother wears a custom-made suit, bold black and white checks, the skirt fitted tight. My sister and I teeter beside her, two untethered buoys, dresses buoyant in the breeze. With her hand shading her eyes, Mother watches the ship, a sailing city crammed with waving couples against a white, white exterior. *Bon Voyage, Bon Voyage*, we cry to friends of Mother's, the wife barely recognizable beneath a veiled hat. Corks burst from champagne bottles; shrieks as the bubbling liquid pours over hands and arms. The ship departs with an exaggerated HONK. We huddle in the back seat of the car. Let's pretend we're sleeping on the ship's deck chairs, we whisper, and imagine the evening growing colder. Perhaps we'd cling together, our shivering bodies wrapped in widely-striped towels. Two girls alone on a boat, the water black and rushing past, lips salty.

New Math

With the roof gone
he peered down
while we ate
Pellets of hail salted the tuna
Matching snowflakes
christened
salads

We were good at math
yet nothing added up
Four minus
one equals three
plus a toothless dog
who gnawed
canned
chicken

A postcard
with no message
arrived damp at the edges
The basement
flooded
again

We prayed
to a god
in a pink negligee
Row like hell, she said
and so we
did

What we'll be

In Mrs. Kelly's fifth-grade class:
six firemen
three teachers
four housewives
the first female President
two policemen
an engineer (the kind that drove a train)
twin veterinarians who liked birds
but would specialize in horses
one fashion model
I was the only hippie

I described a wedding I witnessed in a park
The bride wore a black dress:
hundreds of pleats, an embroidered
field of poppies
The groom donned denim
After the vows, the guests
tossed brown rice

I imagined the hippies' lives:
a million sunflowers
and three pink babies.
Their family nothing like mine:
One housewife
One daughter
One salesman long gone

Chanukah

David's Buick is packed with so many stuffed animals it looks like he's robbed a zoo. At his ex-wife's house, he opens the car door, wrestles a full-size tiger out by its tail and drags it across the snow-covered lawn. It takes 20 minutes to fill the den with damp toys. Laughter shrill, smiles too wide, his daughters roll atop the plush mountain of new pets. They hope this year's performance will convince Dad to stay. Last Chanukah was such a failure.

Annie never minded waiting for her friend. A few minutes alone in a café with nothing more than coffee, a book and her thoughts revived her. She sipped, enjoying the murmur of conversation from nearby tables, and the slant of milky morning light on the wooden floor. Besides, her friend Isabel, with her evolving hairstyles, was worth the wait.

Isabel arrived 15 minutes late. Her hair, last worn in a dense black cloud, now towered in a teased and sprayed cone, several feet above her head. Annie wondered if something was secreted inside this new creation—a small drawer for spare change? Maybe what hovered above her friend's heart-shaped face was a hive.

In the woods, not far from a road where Annie rented a cabin, was The Buzzing Bush Apiaries. Droning captives filled the apiary's crude pine boxes. Nailed to a tree hung a hand-written sign: "Please respect the girls." Annie had never considered the bees' gender. There was the queen, but "queen" seemed less about sex than attitude. The hive's RuPaul, glittering yellow and black stripes and a diamond-studded stinger.

Oblivious to her friend's thoughts, Isabel launched into a tale about her father. The friends explored the "whose father is the worst" theme obsessively. Of all the lousy dad stories they shared, Annie's recollection of an early childhood Christmas card was hard to beat.

Tearing open the plaid envelope, Annie had found an oversized card with "Greetings from the Clarks" in sparkling red script along its top. Below it was a glossy family portrait of her grinning father and stepmother wearing Santa Claus hats and candy cane sweaters. In each of their laps sat a matching Yorkshire terrier. Isabel agreed that Yorkies as stand-ins for Annie and her sister was an insult, but, she insisted, her father was worse. Not once did he tell her she was pretty, and that trumped anything.

Annie, still in her RuPaul daydream, imagined the entertainer in a giant blond wig. She wondered if, like her friend, his hair reflected some unresolved parental hurt.

"Cool hair," said the waitress to Isabel.

"She always looks pretty," said Annie.

A teary-eyed Isabel took her friend's hand. "You know," she said. And, of course, Annie did.

Swing

It begins with
the older girls' voices,
meant to cower
then your own cries
tinny   floating

Your hands
small knobs of ivory
untouched by history
the girls a helix
above as you
climb the hill
settle on the thread-bare
hammock of the swing's
seat, chains chilled against

fingers. The girls push push
then flee   hooting   stumbling
to the street
in love with leaving you
just as your

toe nudges a cloud
and you scream, one
shot of pure elastic pleasure
   Look!

1968

After the cartoon's jittery black and white title,
the nervous sax riff, I push aside fifth-grade
math, move closer to the T.V. for the first reveal
of the bulldog's massive ears. My breath

quickens at his heavy lids, mile-wide collar
mountained with studs, the shoulders outlined
in electric black, barely contained within the screen.
Glimmering

in the background a kitten, tiny-pawed
pert-nosed, a long-lashed fleck
of feminine allure. When the animals draw
closer, lock eyes

swamp stink drifts from the moist
trenches beneath my arms.
I can't explain
the sudden dampness

or how I know the dog's sobs
as the kitten kneads a soft fur nest
in the center of his back
mean pleasure as much as pain.

I have no words for the couples float
to the ceiling on a raft
of pink fluff, or why they snore
so serenely on their descent.

I only know the animals' union
describes an adult world, lush and dark.
If I need a reason to grow up
it is this.

Three Bedrooms in New Jersey

1.

My mother insists my bedroom was pink, but I recall the pale gray wallpaper printed with delicate ballerinas. I think I'm correct in my recollection; when I'm daydreaming I see my small finger tracing the outline of a dancer. One autumn, a neighbor removed the hanging seats from his daughter's swing set and trussed a deer he had shot to the top bar. I could smell it as I lay in bed.

2.

We abandoned the little ranch house for a charmless split-level in a new development. Divided into two tiers of clunky rooms, the foyer sported a marble floor and, whenever it rained the basement filled with water. My bedroom was painted lavender and I loved the furniture: a white desk and bed edged in gold, its canopy draped with pink ruffles. I'd arrange toys atop the fabric, and when the lights were out, look up at the sky I'd fashioned: dark blobs of stuffed bears and tigers, the rectangular shapes of sanitary napkins, swiped from my mother's bathroom. Perfect mattresses for Barbie and Ken.

3.

After my father moved in with his girlfriend, my mother sold the split-level and rented a two-bedroom in an apartment complex rife with divorced mothers and the under-employed. I shared a small, dirty-white room with my sister. One closet held our clothes. At night, feral cats in the bushes wailed like the witches in Macbeth. I once opened the window and shouted, "Shut up!" They stopped humping and gnawing on birds to stare, eyes yellow-green in the streetlights.

I've Blown Out My Shag Haircut

What's all this?

We're sitting in Billy's parents' basement on these plaid couches that smell like his 5 brothers' farts when Beau puts his arm around me. First I'm like *ew* because of Beau's B.O. & then I move closer & rest my head on his shoulder because, well, B.O. or not it's Beau & it's so cool that maybe Beau & I could be a couple like Sue & Billy. Sue & Billy have been together 6 months. People are looking at Beau & me then looking at each other because Beau's done this before, acted like he likes me. Like the time a bunch of us did a séance. We contacted Beau's Grandma. Beau said he could smell her talcum powder & then Beau & I went in a bedroom & made-out for a long time. & once we met in a park when no one was around & played Crazy Eights on the make-out table & then we made-out even though the make-out table was for couples who had been together for 2 weeks or more. So the guys look & the girls pretend not to. Then Saturday Night Live is on & Gilda is Emily Litella. Her hair's a big ball of frizz & she's wearing clear dork glasses & one of those old lady sweaters closed really tight at the neck with a big pin, & she's pissed off. This time it's about "violins" in movies. She's pounding her fist on the desk & saying, "What's All This I Hear About Violins In Movies!" Bill Murray tries to stop her, "Miss Litella!" he says. He wants her to know that it's not VIOLINS in movies it's VIOLENCE in movies & just when she's about to say, "Oh. Well. That's different," this dim-wit Mitchell looks first at me & then at Beau & in his mouth-breathing way says, "Beau, dude. What are you doing with Emily Litella?" Beau looks at me and lets out this fake horror movie shriek like I had somehow snuck under his arm without his knowing it. & then everybody's laughing. I just sit there blinking, but inside I'm repeating Emily Litella's famous line, "Never mind. Never mind. Never mind."

Mother and I peer down from behind the torn screen of the kitchen window as the twins run across their lawn and onto ours. Their hair—neon white in the sun—cut Dutch boy-style over too small ears.

"Hell-woe," they call, thick tongued. The neighborhood "retards."

Mother bounces on her toes, pointing. "Haw… haw…" She's trying to laugh but that muscle is rusty.

"Look!" one twin yells. Pushing, staggering, they run to the bushes near our back door.

Mother's a blur in a sour housecoat, slippered feet pounding the stairs, me racing behind.

A twin drags a dead cat from beneath a bush by its rigid paw. Skinny, gray, a scabbed-over eye; like any stray. Mother wraps her arms around herself, rocking back and forth. Wipes her leaking eyes with the back of her hand.

The twins stare at each other, then Mother. "We get you new cat! We give you cat! Tomorrow! Tomorrow!" They run away, proud to have found a solution.

That night, I awake to Mother's steps creaking across my bedroom floor. She's crying again. Over the damn cat. She wants me to hold her, stroke her hair.

"Tell me," she says, lifting the sheet and lying down, shoving her wide back against me.

"It's fine, Mother," I say, as I always do. "Everything is fine."

Table Talk

My mother tells her friend on the phone about my father's latest misdeeds: he's lost money at the track, meant for my brother's tenth birthday party, a no-big-deal family thing at a diner, but still. Her voice gets screechy as she talks of the boy he was caught fondling in the bathroom of a bowling alley. The worst part: the dumb schmuck doesn't even bowl. I don't need to hear the flat *ah-has* and *hmms* of the listener to know she's not interested. Mother sits at the dining room table, legs thrust underneath, a filmy nylon nightgown brushing her knees, her calves dry and scratched. I'm stretched out beneath the table watching her feet rub together like another pair of fussing hands.

Mall Flower

I've blown out my shag haircut
and it's big.
BIG-big. Cool

With the mirrored halter-top
and jeans chopped into shorts.
SHORT-shorts.
I'm psyched for the mall

And its food court, where I strut
the aisles on swizzle
stick legs
past Jahn's green whipped cream,
past Beefsteak Charlies,
past the crepes at Magic Pan,
past the Nut Shoppe's chocolate
turtles

To buy cigarettes at Mr. Pipe
where Scott wears an afro
and a Star of David,
ties a red bandana
to the loop of white overalls,
and asks me to meet him
behind Cinnabon
where I wait, back pressed
against cinderblocks,
face tilted to the sun,
knowing, as I suck
the smoke in deep,
that I'm a fox.
A   total   fucking   fox.

"Dad's a dick," my sister said.

I turned to see him throw $20 on the candy counter for one small bag of popcorn. "Keep the change," he told the girl. Of course, she was cute and, like, 16. Then he sat there, eating it all and fidgeting. I wasn't surprised when he got up 10 minutes into the movie mumbling something about too much blood and gore.

"Get me a box of Junior Mints," I told him.

Float to Water

I don't remember the name of the boy in high school
or if I cried at his funeral
careful not to smear mascara
hoping after the priest spoke of God's will
weeping girls vowed friendship in the afterlife
I'd be beneath the arm of a boy
in a paneled basement
too stoned not to laugh

I remember potato chips' greasy aftermath
girls' patchouli   guys' sweat
the boy in high school's pink scalp beneath thin hair
train track of ribs
as wind lifted him in the parking lot
tumbling   arms flapping to entertain

The girl who sat beside him on the bridge
the end of her joint blinking, said
after his hat   scarf   plaid jacket
his jump was just like that day in the parking lot

     Arms   spread   wide

         floating

         to

         water

Your Last Rooster

Honeycomb

There were trees,
and beneath them
an apiarist's bee box,
ugly in its simplicity,
with slits for windows.
An abandoned,
three-tiered tenement.

I had wondered about bees
in those boxes, their industry
so directed: The queen,
black wings glittering,
adored and loathed.

My eye to a slit:
No bustling inside.
No extruded amber.
Wings onyx straight jackets.
A low hum of displeasure.

I once lived in an apartment
with too many roommates.
One initialed each egg
in its carton.
Another swigged scotch
till she stung.

I think of us now
in that warren of rooms,
our droning lives.
How small we became
to fit there.

Your Last Rooster

You half hoped the cartoon
cock-a-doodle-do,
that startled you at daybreak,
had come from the man
in your bed
who'd strutted about the bar,
over-preened chest
atop short bent legs.

He'd promised another go round
with you, the evening's choice hen.
Vowed to cook pancakes in the morning.
But his muscles fluttered
and off he flew
leaving the stink of barnyard
on the sheets.

The cock crowed in the alleyway,
again and then again.
You parted the curtain.
Peered through the glass.
Hoping for him—
russet beak, legs spinning.
Anything but the reflection
of your own sooty eyes,
hair a bale of dry hay.

You huddled on your side of the bed and I on mine as we watched a bird outside our window spy on you. An ordinary pigeon, it perched on our sill, swiveling its head.

"Quiet!" you hissed. "It's listening."

I looked at the bird and then at you, with your broad back shoved against the wall. "I don't think it's a spy," I said. "It's not wearing a trench coat or sunglasses."

You made that prissy tisk-tisk sound. Tisk-tisk. You don't understand. You don't understand. Again. I didn't understand that you held secrets of interest to that bird. I didn't understand that if you called my friends a "bunch of Lesbos," you did it to protect me. Why, you wondered, couldn't I recognize their seductive ways, or acknowledge your act of heroism? You were baffled when I wouldn't let you kiss me, after you took my young face in your hands, and with a finger drew lines on either side of my mouth. "Old," you had whispered. I didn't understand, you said with a hoot, that it was hard to get hard when my ass was soft.

I arose and peered through the glass at the feathered sleuth. "I was wrong," I said. "There is something suspicious about that bird." I wanted to offer a moment of understanding before I left. Because I did understand. Finally. "Yes, I was wrong," I said, not to the man whimpering on the bed, but to the you I remembered, the you who would have laughed at the thought of a spying bird.

A New Tattoo

I'm shoveling the driveway while my boys play on our snow-covered front yard. "Asshole," the little one says, as a snowball hits him on the chest. We've been okay, my sons and me. Then my wife shows up. I swear I can smell her perfume—roses and burnt candy—before I see her coming. Ice crunches beneath the wheels of my car she "borrowed," and something loose rattles in back. She's waving, *Hey, I'm home!* Like nothing's happened. Like weeks haven't passed since she left. We stand there, frozen in our spots. She pulls up to the curb and lowers the window. With a big, fake pout she asks the boys, "Aren't you happy to see your mom?" They look at me like they're asking, *Can we Dad?* I shrug. What am I supposed to do? Tell them not to love her? The door opens and she steps out. As she bends to grab her coat off the seat, I see a new tattoo, I think it's an eagle, above her ass. Out come the gifts—her disappearing acts always end with gifts—a Game Boy and a fancy science kit wrapped in plastic with their price tags still on. The kids take a few steps toward her; they'd run if I wasn't watching. She pulls them closer. One son has his head against her shoulder; the younger boy's arms are wrapped around her hips. I hate myself for wanting to be where he is. My hand right on that eagle where it's warm.

Tuscaloosa

A pin stuck in a doll's heart
then one in its foot.
Hot vapor with its own populace:
The cashier at Stop & Shop
with the dead eyes and gray perm.
Your neighbor's pick-up truck.
Grandpa's house with grandpa inside,
and a prom queen wearing a fake
satin dress, her corsage pinned just so.
Beloved for its years of service,
a Ferris wheel gently rocks its riders,
then dumps them to the ground.
People laugh at the banality
of final thoughts.
Closer to the stars a man finds
comfort recalling the part
in his daughter's hair.

Her Hair, a Braid

Lips wavy in the chrome teapot's reflection,
you mouth for-ty, slowly, and again,
for-ty, as if it were a word discovered,
not the years since your mother's death.

Would it help if I mention the boxes
in the basement? Her braid is there,
loosely wound beneath sepia
tissue paper, a part of her
to worry in your fingers.

I want to tell you I wore a coat
today with a fur collar
like your mother's mink pelts.
Black and oily, they smelled
of crowded ships and herring,
wood smoke on snow.

Still Life with Road Kill

Spooled across the dirt road, the bear,
dead. A malodorous, spent planet.

I smelled its hold-your-breath,
kick-to-the-gut of life
stopped short. Whirring atop
its flattened skull's tire-track
tattoo, an unlucky wreath of flies.

I stood near the bear, hand
on chest. Not in some form
of prayer, but to press back
what had lain still.

I had a boyfriend who was struck by a car.
His death arrived like a gift.
I had wanted him to die.
His rage gobbled color,
blotted sound.

I thought of him afterwards
with a kind of shorthand:
Our legs beaded with lake water
His aversion to birds,
then beans. How good food
tasted when he wasn't there
to share it.

The bear was left on the road to rot.
It seemed undignified, the menace
reduced to a malingering mass.
Now I see the wisdom
in its slow surrender.
Why bury what will never stay dead?

No Word for Enchantment

My aunt no longer recalls the word pond.
She would not recognize her reflection—
opal face, fanned lashes on rouged cheeks,
a glamorous sea creature in violet perfume.

At the pond, I skipped a stone
that pinged a frog's face.
She no longer recalls its slow eyes.
Gone is the word for enchantment.

She who walked a city block in seconds,
cashmere-covered elbows a blur of purpose,
waits for the scratchy, long-distance voice
of a mother gone fifty years.

Imagines her husband
whose mouth she's kissed a million times—
a burgler   the postman

Once she told stories of a Parisian childhood:

   amber ablaze in a dollhouse bedroom
      pale garters hoisting seamed stockings
         bad shrimp in Provence

Now she asks:

Why haven't you brought me a small black dog?

Find Me

I told my friends my father had joined the circus. Then I wrote a story about it. Now I read the story to remember my father.

I told people:
    I put my tongue in the mouth of an old man who winked at me
    I wore silk underwear then returned it to the lingerie shop
    I pierced the nipple of a carny in his ring-toss booth
    I spent a night in a motel in Albuquerque: One mustache hair
    on the bathroom mirror. Something about a bearded lady
(I think some of that is true.)

My jobs:
    McDonald's: Terrible acne from French fry machine
    Bloomingdale's: Towel department
    Baby sitter: Painting of a couple embracing in a misty pastel cloud
    Lifeguard: Removed lining from swimsuit (translucent when wet)
    Nut Shoppe: Never cleaned inside of soft-serve machine
    Design studio: Many conversations concerning shades of black
(Possible employment. Or stories told to me.)

I wore:
    A necklace strung with crystals from the dining room chandelier
    A metallic jumpsuit cinched with an alligator belt
    Hot pants and no top
    A blouse inspired by Princess Diana's wedding dress
    Sky blue mules topped with feathers
(My outfits or clothing worn by friends and celebrities.)

Vera, a pink planet spanning the width of two hands, was born.
(This is true.)

Party at my Place

Continuing Ed.

Joan arranges neat rows of pastels
Susan and Sally squeeze whirls
of cobalt and saffron
Eugene steadies a sketchpad on his easel
The new model, Ashley, arrives
Luca, the instructor, says, "Ashley is awesome"
All the models—Madison and Addison
Shaniqua and Samantha
Taylor, Tyler, Chelsea and Chantal—
  are "awesome"

Eugene stares at Ashley
Robert stares at Ashley
Pat, Pam and Peggy stare at Ashley—
reclined, an odalisque on a velvet love seat
Her haircut—shaved on the sides,
long on top—
is nothing new
The students yawn at studded tongues
tattoos of squirrels, skulls and snakes
a nipple ring is one more piece of jewelry

What Joan and Joyce
Susan and Sally
Robert, Eugene, Pat and Pam
haven't seen is a model so bare
Ashley has no pubic hair

Robert and Randal recall daughters
as children and look away
Pat, the minimalist, draws a "v"
anchors it with a vertical line

Peggy moves her easel
to the back corner of the room
reaches her hand
inside the elastic of her slacks

and rests it—not in a sexual way
she's past that—
but to feel the spring of hair
beneath cotton underpants
black, verdant and untamed

Woodstock Duet

To Wed

At the flea market where we buy candles shaped like fairies and soap that wafts patchouli, a man sits in a wheelchair. He wears an old black tux, shiny at the elbows, his gray hair styled and sprayed into a fragile tornado. On his lap sits a Chihuahua wearing a bridal outfit—veil and all. No one notices the couple, except us. We can't stop staring at them staring into each other's eyes, so much in love.

Pa & Ma

Pa Woodstock pushes Ma Woodstock in a makeshift rickshaw down Tinker Street. They're tree-like, all twisted limbs and rough-hewn bark. Pa is the taller tree; Ma is smaller, but they look the same, especially with their long beards. The rickshaw is a monument on wheels to Ma, who waves at gawkers, a beauty queen on a float of faded flowers. With its black-light posters taped to the sides and tie-dyed rags fluttering, the rickshaw is a scrapbook too. A rickety remembrance of the time Pa and Ma lived large, their house a patchwork of barn wood, a misshapen chimney emitting drifts of pot smoke.

Wool and Spool

The poets in my workshop are meeting without me. I heard the news from a former member who spotted me weeping in a wine bar and just had to tell. They've started their own workshop "Two Days of Joy," that is not a workshop at all but an invitation-only-BDSM-LGBT-furry friendly-little people-giants-welcome-NAMBLA tolerant-weekend-sex-athon held in the tent of an abandoned circus. The other members, apparently too busy juggling Ben Wa balls and buying backless Spanky skirts, never mentioned the change in plans.

To: Aimee@Domedirty, Pam@pettingzoo, Tamara@tiemeariver, James@giantisonlyhalfofit, Deirdre@godownwarddog, Bob@ofhumanbondage

Subject: Thanks for the invitation to "Two Days of Joy."

I don't know what I did to deserve this brutal abandonment, but let me tell you: I will never, and I mean NEVER!! allow you to read my rhyming sonnets again. Not even the new piece. The one you said:

Oh, yes, I can't wait for that.

In case you've forgotten, it's about my mother knitting an afghan. I will tell you there's a lovely near-rhyme at the beginning: wool and spool. Think about that next time you're doing Miss Kitty. You just think about that.

Water Witched

We sat at a bar and talked
about lovers' feet.
He once had a girlfriend
with feet like a geisha:
carved ivory, silken and cool
in his palms.
I had slept with a man
who wore a strapped-on leg.
The foot was Band aid-colored.
Near the bar, swans
with sour expressions
drifted in a wading pool.
He pointed to their black feet,
then to his own big toe,
webbed to the one beside it.
He called it a divining rod.
He had used it to find me.

Peonies

Not far from our new house in the country sits another house, a glorified trailer with an overstuffed flower garden. I drive past and wave enthusiastically to the owner, red-faced from his labors, who returns the gesture with equal zeal. Early in the evening, I decide to visit my neighbor. I choose clothing carefully: a flowered blouse, perfume. I'm not sure why. Besides the wave, he isn't attractive: wispy strands of black hair barely stretch across an oversized head. A droopy stomach over droopy shorts. I find him beside his house, in a shed lit with a single bare light bulb. *I'm here for the peonies*, I say. We look at each other for a long moment. Up close, his nose is blunt. A fine white scar divides the bottom lip. *Peonies*, he says slowly, as if I've uttered the correct password.

Life of Charlotte

Teenage Bride

The bride wore a white polyester gown with a train that extended out
the door of the church and down the block. Years later, she blamed
the soiled fabric for the failure of her marriage.

Wall of Icons

A wall of icons can be beautiful if you don't look closely at the hands.
The hands tell stories of too short lives and unrequited love.

Eclipse

The neighbors gathered around the television to observe the moon do
a slow striptease. Having waited so long, the moon wanted its moment
in the sun.

Oh no

She opened the bathroom door and watched the comb and brush
jump apart.

The Shopkeeper

I return to the furniture shop to purchase the chair I had admired earlier that day. A butterfly chair, the owner had said, pointing to the wing-like curves of its metal frame, the long slope of leather. No light is on outside the shop. When I peer closely through the window, I see the hazy glow of a small lamp. The owner may be inside. The door is unlocked. I step into the cool mustiness of the dark space, then move cautiously around small tables, a heavy cardboard box, until the light and what it illuminates becomes visible: the shopkeeper, in an olive-colored tunic, sleeps on an orange and brown plaid couch. His eyes are closed yet restless, as if too many thoughts loop beneath the lids. Behind him, a small phonograph plays a lazy jazz saxophone. It's too intimate: the sensual music; watching the man sleep; his bare legs. When I turn to leave, he opens his eyes. "Stay," he says. Hand over hand, he reels me in.

wake me with skittering nails on the roof. I thought country squirrels would be fat fluffs of fur snoring in tree knots like hung-over frat boys. But they won't sleep. Neither will my cousin and his wife whose bed squeaks at 3 a.m. and 3:10, 3:30 and 4. He with the beard and belly; she with permed hair; who regal us with stories of grandchildren's softball leagues, baby Ella's pigtails.

I thought my husband and I were different too, with our ironic quips and narrow black clothing. And it would be us, oblivious to others' sleep, rocking the bed for an hour, early Sunday morning.

White Legs

I imagined you, a grown man in a tiny kimono, its obi
no bigger than your navel. Your hand with its perfect
oval nails cupping a bowl—eggshell thin and pale as a dew drop—
while you poked toothpick-sized chopsticks into fish
porridge and sperm-shaped beans, lotus roots carved
with clunky holes, like a mouse's drawing of Swiss cheese.
If the mouse were to render your legs they'd be white
and as skinny as soba noodles stretching to the top of the page.
The mouse would laugh at the way the noodles sliced the paper
in two and congratulate itself for using the negative space so wisely.

You're Coming With Me

If I should die,
I want you to die too,
so we could be alone in the morning
and sleep 'till 12,
King and Queen Tut entombed.

Egyptians preferred a bigger brood,
extended family, pets and slaves.

Let's leave them all behind.
The kid's busy with her boyfriend.
Our parents, too old to care.

I'd free the bird and bag the cat.
No one would want him anyway,
staring blankly as we babble:
My god, how he loves us.

Let's leave the cockroaches,
neighbor's flooding bathtub,
3 am regrets.
I wish I had, we say
to the other's sleeping back.
For what? Well,
we could fill hours.

What missteps with this coda?
Etch our story in hieroglyphics.
Crowns tilted at unflattering angles,
togas tight,
our feet pointing east
toward life.

Party at my Place

My vagina invites you to a party
whenever your time frees up
or now,
now would be better.

You see, it remembers the evening
when it left your apartment.
A pack of dogs followed it home.
The neighborhood tomcat,
balls bouncing,
scaled the fire escape,
sprayed the bedroom window.

You wouldn't recognize my vagina now,
it's so well behaved.
Sitting for hours on an office chair,
wearing cotton underpants,
while it yearns for the days
of trimming and perfume.
A walking florist's shop
with the sign swinging.

No need to r.s.v.p.
or bring anything.
Just get here.
The cat's at the window
and dogs circle the block.

About the Author

Tina Barry's food, style and relationship articles appear in newspapers, magazines and online. Her poems and short fiction can be found in *Drunken Boat, MadHat Lit, Lost in Thought, Inch Magazine, The Orange Room Review, Elimae,* and *Exposure, an anthology of microfiction* from Cinnamon Press (2010), among other publications. Barry holds a Masters of Fine Arts degree from the creative writing program at Long Island University, Brooklyn. After living for three decades in Brooklyn, NY, she now makes her home in the Hudson Valley. Contact Tina Barry at tbarrywrites@gmail.com.

Acknowledgements

Thanks to Robin Stratton, my writing Fairy God Mother. Thanks to all the teachers who challenged, praised and pushed, especially Joanna Fuhrman and her workshops, where so many of the pieces in *Mall Flower* originated. Thanks to Barbara Henning, who jump-started and helped hone much of the writing; and thank you to all the professors at Long Island University, including Jessica Hagedorn, Deborah Mutnick, John High, Lewis Warsh, and Alex Mindt. I'm grateful to Jo Ann Beard, who cheered me on early in my writing career, as did Stephanie Elizondo Griest, Nancy Kelton and Susan Bono. To my friends Deirdre Sinnott, Rozanne Gold, Cathy Arra, Jan Elliott, Aimee Herman, Judy Pierce, Bonnie Cooper, and everyone who slogged it out with me in so many writers' groups: Where would I be without you? And thanks to my long-time friend and employer James Girone.

I'm grateful for the support of my sister Tamara Ehlin, whose intellect and kindness inspires me. My daughter Anya Barry's beauty and humor inspires me. I'm lucky to have my family: Barbara Danin, Alex Danin and Faye Miller, constant lights in my life. And Bob Barry, my guy always.

Made in the USA
Las Vegas, NV
28 December 2022

64295320R00038